Fraser Megan

Mum

Valentina

Claudius

Cuthbert

Mayor
Silverbottom

ROME

Vatican City

Hotel Rosso

Basilica di Santa Maria in Trastavere

River Tiber

Spanish Steps

Trevi Fountain

Museum

Claudius' piazza

Pantheon

Colosseum

Roman Forum

For the even more splendiferous Nola and Sienna

OXFORD
UNIVERSITY PRESS

Great Clarendon Street, Oxford OX2 6DP
Oxford University Press is a department of the University of Oxford.
It furthers the University's objective of excellence in research, scholarship,
and education by publishing worldwide. Oxford is a registered trade mark
of Oxford University Press in the UK and in certain other countries

British Library Cataloguing in Publication Data

Data available

ISBN 978-0-19-275880-4

1 3 5 7 9 10 8 6 4 2

Printed in China

Paper used in the production of this book is a natural,
recyclable product made from wood grown in sustainable forests.
The manufacturing process conforms to the environmental
regulations of the country of origin.

HORACE
& Harriet

Friends, Romans, Statues!

**WRITTEN AND ILLUSTRATED
BY THE SPLENDIFEROUS**

CLARE ELSOM

OXFORD
UNIVERSITY PRESS

Lord Commander Horatio Frederick
Wallington Nincompoop Maximus
Pimpleberry the Third

THE HELPFUL BIT BEFORE WE START PROPERLY

This is Lord Commander Horatio Frederick Wallington Nincompoop Maximus Pimpleberry the Third. But that's an awful lot to remember, so you can just call him Horace, for short.

And that's me, sitting right next to him.

Horace is the one who looks like a statue, because, as you might well know by now, Horace *is* a statue. And he's almost 388 years old.

I'm Harriet. I'm the one who's *not* a statue and I'm seven and seven-eighths years old.

1

Then there's Grandad. He's the one who looks like a grandad. Mum says I shouldn't really talk about how old other grown-ups are, because they don't like it. (But I will tell you it's *pretty* old.)

And there's Barry. He's the one who looks like a pigeon. Because he's a pigeon.

And Tiger is the one who looks like a dog, because he's a dog. Not a Tiger. I don't *think* Mum would let me get a Tiger, even though that would be Totally Awesome ... it took me seven years to convince her to let me get a dog. Called Tiger.

So anyway, when I say that Horace is a statue, he's not just an ordinary, staying still, behaves-himself-and-doesn't-cause-any-trouble statue. Horace is a *little* bit out of the ordinary.

Horace has a lot of what he likes to call Great Adventures. I call them Horace Situations. Grandad prefers to call them What-In-The-Name-Of-Bearded-Bernard-Has-He-Managed-To-Do-Now Incidents.

For example, there was the time that Horace added cannons and a moat to

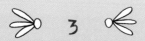

Grandad's shed. They're still there now
actually. Grandad and I really like our
early morning row in the moat.

Or the time he got a job as a journalist
and somehow made the whole town start
wearing ruffs around their necks.

And the time that Horace *almost* became the world record holder for Bestest Ever Shotput.

And then there was the time I went to Italy and … well, actually, that's the time I'm going to tell you about right now.

So, what I should really be saying to you is:

Ciao amici!

That means 'hello friends' in Italian. I know that because I looked it up in our guidebook to Rome, which is the capital city of Italy. And the reason that we had a guidebook to Rome, which is the capital city of Italy, was because we were GOING TO ROME, CAPITAL CITY OF ITALY!

When I say 'we', I mean Mum and Grandad and I. We were going to visit

Mum's best friend Becky, who moved to Rome last year.

Tiger had to stay behind, which I was a bit sad about, but my amazing friends Fraser and Megan had to stay behind too, so they were going to be looking after him. I wasn't sure Megan's cat was very excited about that, but I hoped they would all be really good friends before long.

I was a teeny bit worried that Horace would feel left out, because he wasn't coming either and it would mean I couldn't hang out with him for a few days. I decided to go and tell him about my Italian adventures.

And that is *exactly* where this story starts.

BIT NUMERAL 1

'… so I can bring you back a present from Rome. And I can send you a postcard! I'll find one with the best picture on it!' I finished telling Horace.

Fraser, Megan, and I had gone to Princes Park after school. We took Horace's favourite chocolate spread and marmalade sandwiches (they were pretty nice, although I preferred peanut butter and banana) which always put Horace in a very good mood.

'*Rome*, you say?' asked Horace, scratching his chin thoughtfully.

Lord Commander Horatio Frederick
Wallington Nincompoop Maximus
Pimpleberry the Third

'And when did you say you were undertaking this voyage, young Harriet?'

'In three weeks' time,' I answered.

'*Three* weeks' time?' Horace repeated. He raised his eyebrows at Barry. Barry winked.

'Yes,' I said slowly, feeling a bit puzzled.

'Well, I daresay you will have a *most* splendiferous adventure! Rome is a truly uncommon city. Had ancestors there myself!' he mused.

He finished off his sandwich and clambered down from his pillar. 'So, how about we play a spot of this Foot-Ball you have been showing me, compatriots?'

'Er, yes, sure!' I said in surprise. 'Megan, your turn in goal?'

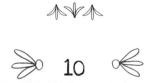

'Well, *that* went well,' said Fraser as we walked home later.

'I know, I thought he'd demand to come along to Rome!' I said. 'Horace usually expects to join in everything.'

'You got off lightly if you ask me,' said Fraser. 'Just think how he would be on an aeroplane—he'd want to fly it himself!'

'Will you send us postcards too, Harri?' asked Megan. 'I wish I was going on holiday!'

'Of course!' I said.

'And bring us back some ice cream won't you? Italians are famous for their ice cream!' said Fraser.

'Er, I'm not sure ice cream will last that long Fraser …' I said doubtfully. 'And anyway, ice cream in Italy is called *gelato*. I looked it up in the guidebook.'

Gelato →

I found out LOADS more things in the guidebook over the next couple of weeks. Like how to say 'thank you' in Italian (*grazie*!) And that Rome had a *whole* museum about pasta. And that gazillions of years ago there was a man called Caesar Augustus who founded something called the Roman Empire, which sounded Pretty Important. And that Ancient Romans wore crazy-looking sandals and helmets called *galeae* and they were really good at building roads.

Caesar Augustus ↓

Pasta ↑

Roman sandals

And that they also invented something called *Roman Numerals* where you don't count in normal numbers like 1 2 3 4 5 6 7 8 9 10 but go I II III IV V VI VII VIII IX X and I think that's *really* cool and I'll probably count like that from now on.

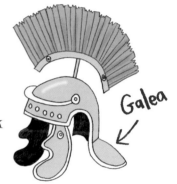

Galea

Before long, there was only a week to go! I thought I would remind Horace that I was going away.

We walked through Princes Park to see him on the way to school.

'I hope he's still in a good mood!' I said. Horace had been surprisingly cheerful for the past couple of weeks. He kept

humming to himself and polishing his
medals and I hadn't seen him yell at the
pigeons once.

'Look, that's odd ... where is he?' Megan
asked, as we approached.

Horace's pillar stood empty. I looked
around.

'Horace?' I called. 'Barry?'

'Maybe he's just gone for a walk or
something,' suggested Fraser.

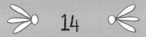

'Maybe …' I said. But Horace not being where he was supposed to be usually meant

he was getting into a Horace Situation.
'Let's come back tomorrow,' said Megan.

But when we Came
Back Tomorrow, Horace
wasn't there *again*.

Or the
next day.

Or the next day.

Lord Commander Horatio Frederick Wallington Nincompoop Maximus Pimpleberry

'This is really weird,' I said, feeling a bit worried. 'Why hasn't Horace told us if he was going somewhere? What if something has happened to him?'

'Oh, something is bound to have happened to him,' said Fraser. 'This *is* Horace we're talking about.'

'Don't worry about it Harri,' said Megan. 'We'll keep checking the park while you're away. You should go, you've got packing to do!'

BIT NUMERAL II

It turned out I was really good at packing.
I was ready for Absolutely Anything.

star chart

beach ball

roller skates

tennis racket

gardening trowel

magnifying glass

ski goggles

Teddy

photo of Tiger

new t-shirt

only the best colour crayons

odd socks

zoo animals

Mum disagreed with some of my
Essential Items For Italy. 'You won't have
time to use all those things, we'll be too
busy sightseeing!' she said as we settled

into our seats on our Really Early in the Morning Flight.

'I like to be prepared!' I said. 'Where do you want to go first, Mum?'

'Well, I'll probably have a *little* catch-up with Becky first ...'

Grandad and I looked at each other in alarm. Mum's 'little catch-ups' usually meant about four and a half days of talking. Which was all the time we had in Rome.

'... but then how about we have a look at

the Colosseum?'

'Yeah!' I said enthusiastically. I knew all about the Colosseum from the guidebook. It was a sort of outdoor theatre called an amphitheatre, and it was built a gazillion years ago. It was older than Grandad. Even older than Horace!

Becky was waiting for us at the airport in Rome, and when she saw Mum, she squealed really loudly, and Mum squealed really loudly and then when Becky saw me she squealed really loudly again and gave me a big hug and said, 'Look how much you've grown!' like all grown-ups do and then they kept chatting and giggling in the car all the way to our hotel and while we unpacked in our room (which had a really cool view of the river Tiber) and while Grandad unpacked in his room

(which had a slightly less cool view of the car park) and then over several cups of *caffè* (that's coffee in Italian) until I was nearly *actually* dying of boredom. Grandad looked at me and waggled his eyebrows and wriggled his nose which was our secret code and I nodded and waggled and

wriggled mine back and we *finally* escaped
to do some proper exploring.

'Phew!' said Grandad as we emerged
blinking in the sunshine. 'How about we
go and see this Colosseum then, Harri?
Maybe after a little *gelato* …?' He pointed
to an ice cream shop.

'Yes!' I said and my mouth fell open at
the sight of all the flavours.

After some Extremely Important
Decision-Making, I had strawberry and
chocolate chip in a cone, and Grandad had
vanilla and honeycomb in a cup.

Rome was completely fabtastic.
Everything was so old! We wandered
through ancient winding streets where
people were chatting across balconies.

We kept coming out into big open
squares called *piazzas* that had statues and
fountains and people playing music.

I stared around one of the big *piazzas*,
just thinking how much Horace would
love to see all this history when …

'THE *INDIGNITY*!' roared a voice.

Grandad and I looked at each other.

'That sounded like …' I started slowly.

'… but it *couldn't* be …' Grandad said,
peering around.

'When I discover which BLUNDERING
DITHERHEAD is responsible for this
abominable treatment! Nobody treats Lord
Commander …'

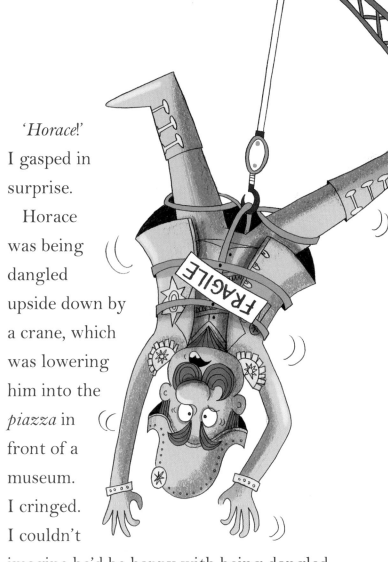

'*Horace*!'
I gasped in
surprise.

Horace
was being
dangled
upside down by
a crane, which
was lowering
him into the
piazza in
front of a
museum.
I cringed.
I couldn't
imagine he'd be happy with being dangled
upside down from a crane.

'Horace!' I called, running over. 'What on earth is going on?!'

'Well, young Harriet, I am VEXED. That is what is going on.'

'But, but … why are you *here*? In *Rome*?' I asked him, as he reached the ground and untangled himself from the harness.

'YOU!' Horace roared at the man operating the crane. 'Are you the blithering idiot responsible for *this*?' Horace turned around and pointed to a sticker on his bum.

'Think that's FUNNY do you?!'

Grandad covered his mouth to hide a smile.

Horace turned to us, brushing himself down. 'I was recently asked to be part of a *most* prestigious international exhibition of world-class statues, with a grand opening in Rome!' he explained. 'I received the intelligence the very same day you informed me of your own passage to Italy. Barry and I resolved to keep it a secret and find you here. I thought t'would be a marvellous surprise!'

'Oh! Well, it is!' I said.

'Especially the fact you kept it a secret …' murmured Grandad.

'On accepting the invitation, I was under the impression I would be sailed on a first-class service to France and thence

28

conveyed across the continent,' continued Horace, 'when in reality I was practically *kidnapped* from my plinth, stowed in a *box*—a BOX for goodness sake—and have spent several horrifying days being shipped as mere cargo!'

'This explains why you weren't on your pillar in Princes Park! I've been really worried,' I told him.

'Well, you were correct to be worried, it's been terrible! Never dreamed I would be treated in this contumely manner. Barry stuck with me of course, the loyal fellow,' said Horace fondly, and Barry fluttered down to Horace's shoulder.

Other statues were being

unloaded around us now. It looked like the exhibition was from all around the world!

'This exhibition is a really big deal, Horace,' said Grandad, pointing at a poster. 'I'm impressed.'

'Of course! It stars me!' said Horace proudly, becoming a bit more cheerful.

Grandad grinned. 'That's the Horace we

INTERNAZIONALE

ROME

know. Well, your grand opening isn't until Sunday. Why don't we go and have a look around Rome together?'

'Yes, and you have to try *gelato* Horace, it's delicious! They have every flavour you can think of!'

'Splendid!' said Horace. 'I'll have a sandwich flavour!'

BIT NUMERAL III

'The last time I was in this fine town, it was 1659,' said Horace, as we strolled towards the Colosseum.

'You've been to Rome before, Horace?' I asked in amazement.

'Forsooth! I was on a terribly important mission for the navy,' he said, puffing out his chest. 'That scurvy scullion Duke Cuthbert Emery Buckington Silverbottom II had visited the previous year, left a dreadful impression of course, so I was sent along to make amends. There was a *small* incident involving a drawing some Italian chap called Leonardo had done ... managed

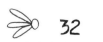

to spill my tea … caused rather a fuss.'

Grandad raised his eyebrows in alarm.

'But that's all forgotten now,' said
Horace, waving his hand. 'Probably why I
was chosen for this exhibition. I occupy a
special place in the hearts of the people of
Rome!'

'You must be pretty pleased to see all
these statues, Horace?' I said, pointing
around a *piazza* we were walking through.
'You've got lots of company!'

'Absolutely!' said Horace, glancing up at

one. 'Although … hang on, what on earth has happened to this poor chap? And … zarbles! Him too!'

He turned to us in horror. 'Where *on earth* are their clothes?'

I giggled. It was true, there were a *lot* of statues with no clothes on!

'It says here that it's a sign of them being athletic or heroic,' said Grandad, reading from the guidebook.

'A sign of being athletic?' spluttered Horace. '*I'm* an athlete, but you didn't see me throwing the shotput IN THE NUDE, did you?'

'No, thank goodness …' Grandad muttered.

'And I shall remain fully clothed for my exhibition, thank you very much!' said Horace primly. 'I must help these poor

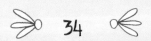

compatriots, post
haste! I mean, not
even a hat, for
goodness sake!'
We were standing
close to a restaurant
with people eating
outside. Horace
grabbed some
tablecloths and
dashed around the square, covering up the
statues. The waiter yelled something in
Italian.

I peered at a statue in the corner of the
piazza with a funny hat. 'Hey, Horace,
this one kind of looks like you!' I said. I
pointed to the label and read out slowly.
'*Claudius Romulus Maximus Pimpleberry ...*'
I swung round in amazement.

'Maximus Pimpleberry? Horace, are you related to him?!'

Horace peered at the statue, 'Aha! Dear old Claudius. Yes, a distant cousin, a rather theatrical fellow! Fitzgibbers, they've practically de-robed him as well!' Horace flung a tablecloth over the statue.

'Horace, this is really cool! Let's get a picture of you together,' I said, and took a picture of Horace with Claudius on Grandad's phone.

We crossed the road to the Colosseum, and had to leap out of the way of mopeds zooming past.

'Zounds! Carriages on my last visit were much more gracious,' said Horace, shaking his head. 'And speaking of clothes—or lack of—the people were in *far* finer attire back then, of course,' he continued.

I rolled my eyes. I was always hearing about The Olden Days and how people used to wear hats and medals and ...

'Although, look at that fine buck and his dashing ensemble!' Horace pointed at someone dressed like a Roman gladiator, who was entertaining the queue at the Colosseum.

'Um, Horace, I think they're actually in costume ...' I said.

'Precisely! Fine costumes! I shall make a trip to the forum!' Before we could stop him he had disappeared into a souvenir shop.

'Behold!' boomed Horace emerging a few minutes later. 'What do you think?'

'Wow. You look … really … um … Roman, Horace,' I said.

Horace beamed.

'Barry! I have bought you a hat, come hither.'

The Colosseum was huge! It was covered in loads of stone pillars and arches and looked fifty hundred times as huge as Stokendale's theatre.

As we were about to join the long queue, a lady came running up to us. '*Sbrigati*! Come on, this way!' she said, and beckoned us through the ticket barriers.

'Er …' I looked at Grandad, who shrugged, so we followed her. Horace, of course, didn't think there was anything out of the ordinary in being ushered to the front of the queue.

'*Sei in ritardo*!' she scolded Horace as we hurried along. 'It's about to start!'

'What's about to start?' I asked, confused.

'You can watch from up there,' she said, and pointed Grandad and me to a balcony running around the edge of the amphitheatre.

'And you, get down there!' she barked at

Horace, pushing him towards the base of the Colosseum, where a platform had been set up over the crumbling floor.

Horace frowned. 'What do you mean by these impertinent orders?!' he asked, crossly.

Just then, a horn blared. '*Signore e signori*, ladies and gentlemen ...' boomed a voice over the loudspeakers, '... we begin!'

Grandad and I watched in amazement as Horace was shoved out onto the platform.

A door in the side of the Colosseum
opened and out ran … a *lion*.

(OK, it was actually a person dressed in
a lion costume, but saying 'a lion' sounds
much more dramatic.)

'What the …?' spluttered Horace in
amazement.

'Grandad, they must think Horace is an
actor! Because of his costume!' I said.

Grandad groaned and muttered
something about this being a What-In-
The-Name-Of-Bearded-Bernard-Has-He-
Managed-To-Do-Now Incident.

'In the first century AD, barbaric
battles between Roman gladiators and
wild animals regularly took place in the
Colosseum ...' blared the voice over the
loudspeakers.

'Oooooh!' said the crowd watching, as the
lion ran towards Horace.

'Now, hold on just a minute!' cried Horace
to the man-lion as he jumped out of the
way. 'Avaunt! Avaunt you fustian feline!'

'Ooh, he's good, isn't he?' said a woman next to me, leaning forward with her camera.

The man-lion charged towards Horace again, who looked Extremely Cross about it and dodged out of the way. 'Now, I have warned you sir … that's quite enough of that! Barry! Attack!'

Barry flew towards Horace.

Uh-oh. I knew what was coming.

'*Ah, dai dai*!' cried the man-lion, as a pigeon poo dripped down his face. '*Per carità*!'

He stopped in his tracks and gestured furiously at Horace.

'… and er, as we see here, this time the gladiator is triumphant! With the use of his, um, Roman pigeon …' said the voice over the loudspeaker.

The man-lion stomped off the platform wiping his face with a towel. There was some uncertain applause around the Colosseum. Horace looked delighted, and bowed to the audience.

'I think it might be time to go Harri,' whispered Grandad, and we hurried towards the exit.

'Horace! Barry!' I hissed, as we raced towards the door, '*Come on*!'

'*Scusa*! Sorry I'm late!' panted a man in full gladiator gear, running onto the

platform. 'Hey, who are *you*?' he said to Horace.

And with that, we raced out of the Colosseum, Horace still bowing and waving to the confused crowd.

BIT NUMERAL IV

'The Colosseum was built in around
70 AD and is the largest amphitheatre
ever constructed ...' I read out from the
guidebook, as we sat down for a snack.

'Why, this is *delicious*!' Horace exclaimed,
taking a huge bite of pizza. 'Better than
sandwiches! Let us introduce this to the

people of Stokendale.'

'We already *have* pizza in Stokendale, Horace. Haven't you ever seen Antonio's restaurant?' I asked him.

'Nay! But I shall be frequenting this Antonio's establishment the moment I return! Another, *per favore*!' he called to the waiter.

'We should warn Antonio about that,' said Grandad. 'Do you want to hear my best Italian jokes, you two?'

'Forsooth!' said Horace.

'No!' I groaned. (Grandad was brilliant at lots of things, but jokes were absolutely not one of them.)

'What do you call a Roman with a cold …?' Grandad began. '*Julius Sneezer*! And what's a Roman's favourite food …? *Caesar Salad*!'

Horace roared with laughter.

I rolled my eyes. (Told you.)

'*Julius SNEEZER*!' Horace chuckled. 'Now, this Caesar fellow. Rather famous isn't he?'

'Pretty famous, yes,' smiled Grandad.

'I rather like the sound of his name,' mused Horace. 'Maybe I should acquire some Roman touches to my name, now I'm a gladiator … freshen things up for the exhibition!'

'You're *not* a Roman gladiator, Horace! And don't you think you've got enough names?' I asked.

'Only a mere six! Although, let it be noted Cuthbert only has four, pah! Anyway … how about Lord *Emperor* Commander Horatio Frederick *Caesar* Wallington Nincompoop Maximus

Pimpleberry the Third,' Horace said, ignoring me as usual. 'Has a nice ring to it, nay? You can all refer to me as such from now on!'

I rolled my eyes again.

'Why don't you write your postcard while we're sitting here, Harriet?' said Grandad.

← gelato

To Fraser and Megan,
Rome is brilliant! We've
seen loads of sights and
it's really hot and I've
had two ice creams
already. And you'll
NEVER guess who we
ran into out here ...
Horace! Say hello to
Tiger from me.
            Harriet xx

Fraser and Mega

4 Clifton Stree

Stokendale

SS4 26N

'Good idea,' I said.

'Finished!' I said.

'Me too!' said Horace.

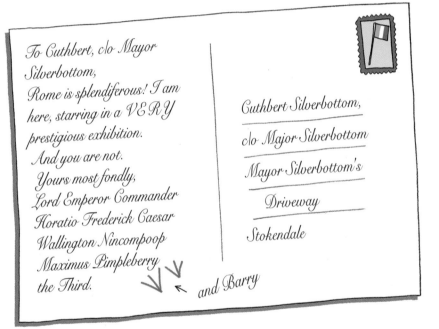

To Cuthbert, c/o Mayor Silverbottom,

Rome is splendiferous! I am here, starring in a VERY prestigious exhibition.

And you are not.

Yours most fondly,

Lord Emperor Commander Horatio Frederick Caesar Wallington Nincompoop Maximus Pimpleberry the Third.

and Barry

Cuthbert Silverbottom,

c/o Major Silverbottom

Mayor Silverbottom's

Driveway

Stokendale

'That's not very friendly, Horace,' I scolded him.

'Well, neither is he!' replied Horace.

'What next, Grandad?' I asked, as we finished our pizza. (Horace had eaten *four* pizzas all to himself.)

'Well, your Mum and Becky won't have even noticed we've left yet,' said Grandad, glancing at his watch. 'So how about we visit the Trevi Fountain? It's one of the most famous fountains in the world. And as they finished building it in 1762, you won't have seen it before, Horace!'

'Let's go!' I said. I was just wondering how soon I could suggest a third ice cream would be A Brilliant Idea when …

'What in name of babbling barnacles is that infernal noise?' Horace said, stopping and staring around him.

'It's opera!'
said Grandad,
and we turned
a corner to see a
woman singing in
the street. She
was acting at
the same time,
wringing her
hands and
gesturing
around
wildly.

'But … great
grimalkins, what on earth is wrong with
her? ARE YOU OK?' Horace bellowed at
the opera singer.

'Shhh Horace! She's meant to sound like
that!' I hissed.

'Preposterous! *No one* is meant to sound like that!' he replied, looking concerned. 'Perhaps she only understands when things are sung to her, ahem …' Horace cleared his throat and then howled, '*DOOO YOOOUUUU NEEED HEEEELP SIGNOOOORA?*' in his own (really bad) impression of opera.

The singer glared at us, and Grandad and I had to drag Horace away. (Again.) 'Well, I was only trying to assist the fair maiden!' grumbled Horace. '*Arrivederci*!'

At the Trevi Fountain there were hundreds of tourists, and lots of people selling things and performing for the crowds.

'It says here if you toss a coin into the
fountain over your shoulder, it guarantees
your return to Rome one day,' Grandad
read from the guidebook. 'Shall we try it?
Stay close Harriet, it's very crowded.'

We lined up in a row next to the clear
blue water. 'One, two, *three*!' I
said, and we all tossed coins
over our shoulders.

'*Mamma mia*!' said a man on the other side of the fountain, rubbing his head and looking confused.

Horace's coin had sailed over the whole fountain. 'Apologies dear fellow!' he called. 'I occasionally forget about my physical prowess!' We stood and watched the crowds, and before long someone threw a coin at Horace's feet. Then someone else did it.

'May I enquire why these mortals are gifting me coins?' asked Horace, puzzled.

I suddenly realised. 'They think you're a performer Horace! There are loads of living statues here, look!'

'Living statues …?' asked Horace.

'Yes! People get dressed and painted

like statues and stand still for ages, and people give them money,' I told him.

Horace looked perplexed. 'People are paid? For being *statues*?! Well, why have *I* not earned my fortune by now?'

'Well, they entertain the crowds as well Horace,' said Grandad. 'Look!'

He pointed at a performer who was painted silver and standing motionless on a plinth gazing towards the fountain. Horace walked up to him and peered closely. 'Well I don't see anything …'

The performer made a sudden movement as if he was going to give Horace a kiss.

'Fitzgibbers!' yelled Horace, staggering backwards. I giggled. The crowds around us laughed and took pictures.

Horace looked completely perplexed.
'Well, they have selected a noble
profession, no doubt, but I do this every
day! I expect to earn a fine bounty from

my exhibition!' he said, and strode to investigate another living statue, who looked like he was hovering in mid-air.

I spotted a woman performer with an amazing costume. She was standing in the corner and wasn't getting much attention. I wandered over to see her. She was perfectly still, and had a bright green bird perched on her outstretched fingers.

It reminded me of Horace and Barry! I dug in my purse for a coin from my holiday spending money, and threw it into her collection pot. The performer stayed completely still, but swivelled her eyes and winked at me, and her green bird bowed. I grinned.

'Hey, come and see!' I turned around to Grandad and Horace … but they weren't there.

There was just a giant crowd of strangers.

'Grandad …?' I called. 'H-Horace?' My voice sounded a bit wobbly.

I hopped up on a nearby bench and looked frantically over the crowd.

'Grandad …?' I tried a bit louder, 'HORACE? *Barry*?'

But they were Absolutely And Completely Gone.

BIT NUMERAL V

I felt my tummy go flippety-flop and I tried to think properly. Grandad always told me that if I got lost I should Stay Where I Was and he would find me.

So I did some Staying Where I Was. I stood on the bench to make myself extra tall. But after *ages* of Staying Where I Was, Grandad still hadn't found me. There were so many people around and it was really hot and I suddenly wanted to be back at the hotel with Mum and Becky more than anything, even if they were doing hours of boring talking. But I couldn't remember where the hotel was.

My tummy flippety-flopped even harder.

'*Scusi?*' asked a kind voice. 'Are you OK?'

It was the performer with the amazing costume that I had just given the coin to.

'H-hello,' I said, 'I-don't-know-where-my-Grandad-is-or-Horace-or-Barry-and-I-think-I-might-be-lost-forever-and-I-don't-know-my-way-around-Rome-and-I-only-know-five-words-in-Italian-and-one-of-them-is-*gelato*-which-I-don't-think-will-help!' I blurted out, and tears splashed down my cheeks.

She sat down on the bench next to me. 'Right. Don't worry about a thing! I can help,' she said soothingly, and handed me a tissue. 'We'll find them. I'm Valentina. This is Bianca,' she said, gesturing to her green bird. 'And Bianca just happens to be fabulously fantastic at finding things.

Why don't you tell me what your Grandad
and Horace and Barry look like, and she'll
have a look?'

'Um …' I said quietly. I knew I
Shouldn't Talk To Strangers, but this
felt like a Proper Serious Emergency, and
Valentina and Bianca looked very kind.

'Well, Grandad looks old and tall and
has glasses and a green shirt. My friend
Horace has a big hat and a moustache and

he's a statue, except at the moment he looks like a gladiator, and Barry … is a pigeon,' I finished.

If Valentina found any of that strange, she didn't say so. Bianca nodded, ruffled her feathers importantly and flew off around the Trevi Fountain.

'I'm Harriet,' I told Valentina. She grinned at me, and shook my hand. We watched Bianca sailing high over the crowds.

'Do you remember where you're staying in Rome, Harriet?' asked Valentina.

'Um …' I screwed up my eyes and tried to remember the name of the hotel. It was written on the red napkins that I was doodling on when Mum and Becky were talking. 'Hotel … R-ro-ro … Rosso?'

'Marvellous macaroni, I know just where that is!' said Valentina. 'It's not far at all. OK, what we're going to do is stay right here for a while and I'm *sure* you'll all find each other. And if not, Bianca and I shall escort you safely to the Hotel Rosso. Does that sound OK?'

I thought about it. It sounded like a good plan.

'Thank you. Yes please,' I said gratefully. 'Am I stopping you working?'

Valentina sighed, 'Oh, it doesn't matter. I never make much anyway.'

'But you're really good!' I told her. 'And Bianca is brilliant, too.'

'Thanks,' Valentina smiled. 'I love performing, but the other living statues

aren't very nice to me.' She stared around the crowds. 'They bully me out of the best spots all over the city, so I get stuck in the corners and can never make enough money. I'll probably have to give it up soon.'

I frowned. 'That's terrible! Why are they so mean to you?'

'I'm not too sure,' said Valentina. 'They say it's because I'm new. But I've been doing this for years now! I expect they're just envious of my hat.' She winked at me.

I smiled. I could still see Bianca searching. She looked like a tiny dot over the other side of the piazza. We waited some

more. And some more. It had been *ages*—where had Grandad gone?

Then I saw Bianca flying back over to us. As she got closer, I saw she had someone feathery with her …

'BARRY!' I cried, as he flew to my shoulder. 'Oh, I am *so* happy to see you!'

Valentina stroked Bianca. 'Excellent work, *piccola*!'

Both birds then flew up again, Bianca hovering above us, and Barry flapping across the *piazza*, looking back at us.

'We should follow them!' I said.

We squeezed our way through the crowds, Bianca guiding us towards Barry. We got to the centre of the *piazza* and …

'H-A-R-R-I-E-T?' boomed a familiar voice. 'Ouch!'

I looked around and saw Horace, standing in the middle of the Trevi fountain with his telescope. He was being pelted with coins as

people threw them into the water to make
their wishes.

There were also several Italian guards
who looked extremely cross and were
yelling and gesturing for Horace to get out
of the water.

'One moment now, I say *one moment*!'
Horace waved them away. 'We must secure
the location of … *Harriet*!' he exclaimed,
spotting me and looking delighted.
'Sterling work Barry!'

'*Harriet*!' cried another voice, and
Grandad appeared through
the crowd, sweeping me into a
huge hug. Grandad looked Extremely
Stressed Out, a bit like the time when I was
four years old and decorated Mum's car with
yellow paint while he had a nap.

'I thought you were right beside me!' he said. 'I had to stop Horace getting into a scuffle with a living statue who tried to steal his hat, then when I turned around you weren't there! I've been going round and round the fountain but couldn't see you in these crowds!'

'It's OK Grandad, I'm fine! Valentina and Bianca looked after me,' I said, and pointed to my new friends.

'*Ciao!*' said Valentina, and grinned. 'I love a happy reunion! Why don't we get out of these crowds and get introduced properly? I'm walking back past Hotel Rosso myself. We could all get a celebratory *gelato* for the road?'

'Excellent idea!' I said, and grinned up at Grandad, holding onto his hand extra tightly.

I introduced everyone to everyone while we picked out *gelato* flavours.

'Honestly, it's no problem!' said Valentina, after Grandad thanked her for the gazillionth time. 'It's a pleasure to meet you all.'

'A fine feathered friend you have there!' said Horace, beaming at Bianca.

'Same to you, Horace!' said Valentina, smiling at Barry. 'Everybody got their cones? Seven scoops enough for you, Horace? Great! I'll give you a little tour while we walk.'

Valentina led the way back to Hotel Rosso. She knew loads about the city. More than the guidebook did! She pointed out the sights and told us stories about Ancient Rome.

'Fascinating!' said Horace, 'It was a sign of leadership to be born with a crooked nose?'

'That's what some people say, yes!' smiled Valentina. 'I could do with a more crooked nose myself, you know. Maybe then the other performers would respect me more!' she sighed.

I told Grandad and Horace about the other living statue performers being unkind to Valentina.

'Maybe a change of scene would help? A different *piazza* maybe?' suggested Grandad sympathetically.

'I've tried *everywhere* in the city!' said Valentina. 'Another performer always shows up and tells me it's their spot. I need to stick up for myself a bit more, I guess.'

We rounded a corner and I saw a *piazza* full of statues wearing tablecloths. 'Hey, we know this place!' I squealed, 'We went

past it earlier! Horace was covering up all the statues!'

'Yes, we're almost there!' said Valentina. 'Hang on, let me just show you this.'

She led us over to a statue in the corner of the *piazza*. 'This is a distant relation of mine,' explained Valentina. 'He's my inspiration for performing, actually. Perhaps, one day, I might do something so remarkable that they make a statue of me. Just like you Horace! But in the meantime, I just love performing as one.' She gazed up at the statue dreamily.

We all stared at Valentina.

Then we all stared back at the statue she was talking about.

It was the statue of Claudius Romulus Maximus Pimpleberry. *Horace's* distant cousin.

'Valentina, what's your last name?'
I asked slowly.

'Hmm?' she asked. 'Oh, it's
Pimpleberry. Valentina
Pimpleberry.'

BIT NUMERAL VI

My mouth fell open.

'Pimpleberry?' squeaked Horace. 'You are a *Pimpleberry*?'

'Yes! What? Why?' asked Valentina, looking around at us all, puzzled.

'Valentina …' I said slowly. 'This statue is also a relation of *Horace's*!'

'Surely not …?' said Valentina, open-mouthed.

'*Yes*!' boomed Horace. 'I am Lord Emperor Commander Horatio Frederick Caesar Wallington Nincompoop Maximus *Pimpleberry* the Third!'

'Well, Horace, that's not *rea* …' I started, '… oh, never mind.'

Horace and Valentina stared at each other.

'Well, I am *flabberfounded*!' said Valentina, at the exact same moment Horace said 'Well, I am *thundersmacked*!'

I giggled.

'I think you two have got some serious catching up to do!' said Grandad.

'It seems that Valentina is dear old Claudius' great great great great great great great great *great* niece!' said Horace proudly.

'And Horace is Claudius' third cousin twice removed!' said Valentina, grinning.

It was the second day of our holiday and we were having breakfast together at Hotel Rosso. Horace and Valentina had been chattering non-stop since their big discovery the day before. They were as

bad as Mum and Becky!

'So … what does that make you two?' I asked, screwing up my eyes in concentration. It sounded very complicated.

They looked at each other. '*Family*,' said Valentina. Horace beamed.

'And it turns out we agree on rather a lot!' said Horace. 'Tis most uncommon.'

'Yes, like *hats*!' said Valentina.

'Simply not worn enough in this day and age,' said Horace.

Valentina nodded wisely. 'And pizza!'

'The finest food around!' agreed Horace.

'And Bianca and Barry have become good friends too,' said Valentina.

'So, what shall we do today?' asked Grandad. 'Your exhibition doesn't open until tomorrow does it, Horace?'

'Well actually,' said Valentina, 'Horace has offered me his expert help. He's going to give me some statue lessons! We're going to go and perform together in the city today.'

'Indeed, I am going to pass on my wisdom!' said Horace, looking proud. 'Make sure you are on top form ready for tomorrow …'

'Tomorrow?' asked Valentina. 'What about tomorrow?'

Horace looked pleased. 'Tomorrow, when you perform at the opening of my exhibition, right outside the museum! I have secured you the spot!'

Valentina's mouth fell open. 'Oh, Horace, *really*? But that's a prime location!'

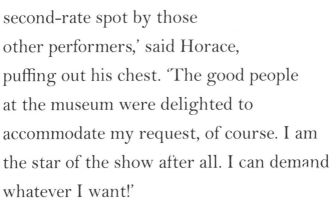

'It certainly is! Only the best for us Pimpleberries! No family of *mine* will be put in a second-rate spot by those other performers,' said Horace, puffing out his chest. 'The good people at the museum were delighted to accommodate my request, of course. I am the star of the show after all. I can demand whatever I want!'

'That's so nice of you, Horace,' I

said. 'Eek, I can't wait to see you *both* tomorrow!'

'Well, we'd better get practising,' said Valentina, finishing her coffee and leaping up. 'Come on Horace!'

They strode out into the Rome sunshine, Barry and Bianca fluttering behind them.

Just then Mum and Becky wandered in for breakfast.

'Morning!' chirped Mum. 'How about we go and see those sights today? Seeing as we didn't get around to anything yesterday! Or did you two have your own adventures?'

Grandad and I looked at each other.

'Sounds great, Mum!' I said. 'Yesterday was pretty quiet, no real adventures. Maybe we can try some *gelato* too …?' I added slyly.

'Of course!' Mum answered. 'A little holiday treat won't hurt.'

Grandad winked at me.

BIT NUMERAL VII

We had a great day with Mum seeing lots more Roman sights. (And there were much fewer Horace Situations when Horace wasn't there.) But Grandad and I were looking forward to seeing the opening of Horace's exhibition, so on Sunday morning we got up super early and walked over to the museum.

There was a huge crowd outside queuing for tickets, and right in the middle were Valentina and Bianca.

'Look, Grandad!' I exclaimed.

The crowds were all smiling and taking photos of the two of them. Valentina's

collection pot was already overflowing
and Bianca was bowing and fluttering her
wings every time a new coin clinked in.
Barry was helping too.

I waved to her as we walked past. 'You
look fabtastic!' I whispered and Valentina
winked at me.

Horace had given us tickets already,
so we walked straight into the museum.
It was *massive*—much bigger than
Stokendale's museum. There were big
pillars and stone floors, and everything
sounded serious and echoey.

We walked past Horace and I gave
him the thumbs up. 'You look awesome,
Horace!' I whispered.

'Indeed I do,' he agreed, nodding
majestically, but staying very still.

'Horace is in Super Serious Statue mode!' I whispered to Grandad.

'Yes, that's the quietest I've ever seen him,' muttered Grandad. 'Maybe Valentina is a good influence!'

We looked around the rest of the exhibition. There were statues from China and Ancient Greece and Russia and Egypt and Africa, and facts about all of the different countries.

Lord Emperor Commander Horatio Frederick Caesar Wallington Nincompoop Maximus Pimpleberry the Third

 93

'Grandad, can we visit all of these places too?' I whispered, staring up at a statue of an African queen.

'Of course! But you'd better start saving your pocket money,' Grandad whispered back.

I also couldn't help but see that a *lot* of the statues had no clothes on. I wondered if Horace had noticed …

We went back out into the sunshine to see how Valentina was doing, and also because it was Definitely Time For Another *Gelato*.

And then Horace came storming out of the museum behind us.

'Ah, knew it couldn't last long …' said Grandad.

'The other statues!' he spluttered indignantly. 'Many of them … *not a stitch* … It's some kind of *nudist* party in there! How can I be associated with such shenanigans? Where are the tablecloths?'

(Horace had definitely noticed.)

'If you could *just* come back inside, Horatio …' pleaded a museum staff member, running out after him. 'We need you to remain on your plinth for the exhibition!'

'Lord Commander *Emperor* Horatio …' said Horace, grumpily.

'Of course … well, if you could *just* come back inside Emperor …'

'I shall not be disrobing, I can tell you that!' blustered Horace.

'No, no, literally nobody wants that,' insisted the staff member. 'How about we move your plinth a little further away from the, er, less clothed artworks?'

Valentina caught the staff member's eye as some coins rattled into her collection pot.

'Oh, Miss Pimpleberry! The museum wanted to pass on how much wonderful feedback we've had for you. You've *really* helped to entertain the queues. In fact, we'd love to offer you a permanent slot here outside the museum. My manager will be out to discuss the details with you later.'

Valentina looked amazed, her eyes shining. 'Oh! Th-thank you! That would be wonderful!' She turned to Horace.

'How can I ever repay you?' she said.

'No need, no need,' Horace waved his hand. 'We Pimpleberries must stick together!'

Valentina laughed happily.

'A relation of mine, don't you know!' Horace said proudly to the staff member as he was ushered back inside the museum. 'The finest living statue in Rome! Well, apart from *myself* perhaps ...'

All of a sudden, it was time to go home.
Horace was still busy with the exhibition,
but Valentina came to
say goodbye while
we waited for a
taxi to the airport.
'Thank you
again!' I said, and
gave her a big
hug. 'I might still
be Completely Lost
Forever if it wasn't
for you.'
'No, thank *you*!'
Valentina said,
hugging me back. 'If I hadn't met you,
I would never have met Horace, and
I wouldn't have my spectacular new
performing spot! Not to mention some

splendiferous new friends.'

I grinned. 'I think you would have come across Horace before too long, he likes to make himself known …'

'I'm beginning to learn that!' she said. 'I'll keep an eye out for him while he's still in Rome.'

'Good luck with that!' said Grandad, shaking her hand.

Bianca chirped a farewell, and we waved them both off.

Mum and Becky were sniffing and hugging and exchanging last-minute stories and saying how little time they'd had to *really* catch up.

(Grown-ups, hey?)

'You'll have to come back to Rome again

soon,' insisted Becky. 'If that's OK with you, Harriet?'

'Definitely!' I said. 'Rome is the *best*. And there are at least five flavours of *gelato* I haven't tried yet!'

BIT NUMERAL VIII

When we finally got back home, I was
a bit sad not to be in Rome any more.
But it was awesome to see Fraser and
Megan and Tiger, who licked me all over
five times. (Tiger, that is, not Fraser and
Megan.)

Fraser and Megan gave me high fives
and tucked into the Italian sweets I'd
brought home for them.

'Mega!' said Fraser. 'Thanks!'

'We got your postcard, too, Harriet,'
said Megan. 'Why on earth *was* Horace in
Rome?'

So I told them everything about

Horace's exhibition and the gladiator costume and the Colosseum and the opera lady and the Trevi fountain and Claudius and Valentina and Bianca and pizza.

'*Woah*!' said Fraser.

'So, he should be back at the end of the month when the exhibition finishes?' asked Megan.

'I think so …' I said.

But it took Horace *ages* to get home.

I got a postcard from him a few days after we got back:

Dearest Harriet,
Greetings from Rome!
The museum has released me from my exhibition commitment early. Something about 'more trouble than it's worth.'. Anyway, I shall not be returning to Stokendale in the same manner of travel as before. I refuse to go through that horror again. Barry and I are going interrailing! Valentina sends her fondest wishes.
Horatio
(and Barry and Bianca)

AIR MAIL

Harriet

Harriet's House

Next to the Cannon Shed

Stokendale

SS5 5CM

Then I got a few more.

Cześć
from Poland

AIR MAIL

Harriet
Harriet's House

And some more, and some more, until I had a massive pile of them:

Then after weeks and weeks and *weeks,*
I finally heard a familiar tap-tap-tap on my
window one morning.

'Barry!' I cried, flinging open the
window. 'You're back! I've missed you!'

He had a note in his beak.

Harriet, we have returned!
Do drop by Princes Park after school.
I have many stories to tell you!

Horatio

PS – any chance of bringing pizza with you?
I would so enjoy some …

THE LAST BIT AT THE VERY END

'He's, er, brought back a few souvenirs then?' asked Fraser, as he, Megan, Grandad, Tiger, and I approached Horace's pillar.

'*Horace*! Welcome home!' I called, and waved.

'My marvellous compatriots! Greetings to you all!' cried Horace. 'How fine it is to see your faces.'

'Hi Horace! We've brought along some pizza!' said Megan. 'We brought quite a

few actually, Harriet said that would be safest …'

'Delightful news!' exclaimed Horace, clambering down from his pillar.

We sat on a picnic blanket and shared out the pizzas and Horace told us all about his big adventures.

'… and then we had to leave Spain— some minor misunderstanding with the *policía*—whereupon we voyaged through the magnificent French countryside, making plenty of agreeable acquaintances along the way of course, and had a *splendid* time in Switzerland and Germany. Barry particularly enjoyed wearing *lederhosen*.'

lederhosen

'Wow. I bet you made some good memories Horace!' I said.

'I bet you left a trail of destruction more like …' said Fraser under his breath, grinning.

'Well, you'll be very pleased to hear that I will be compiling my 14,962 photographs into an informative lecture for you all! It should be ready within the week,' said Horace, looking proud.

We all looked at each other in alarm. 'Oh … great!' I said, crossing my fingers and wondering How I Could Get Out Of That.

We started on the seventh pizza.

'So Horace, what's your next plan?' I asked. 'Are you going to be travelling anywhere else?'

I was really happy that Horace had such a great time away from Stokendale, and

especially that he'd met Valentina. But it turns out I actually missed him and Barry quite a lot when they were gone. Life was always just a *little* bit more interesting with Horace around.

'Well,' pondered Horace. 'I was contemplating this on our passage home. I must say, while Barry is *excellent* company, I did rather miss my other Stokendale chums. I think I shall be

staying put for a while.'

He looked fondly at us all. 'Perhaps we can share our next adventure *together*?'

'Yes!' said Fraser.

'Definitely!' said Megan.

'Yip!' barked Tiger.

'If we must …' muttered Grandad.

'Forsooth!' I said, grinning up at him. 'That sounds *splendiferous*, Horace.'

FINE

(That means 'The End')

PHRASEBOOK

ARRIVEDERCI!
Goodbye!

BIANCA
White

CAFFÈ
Coffee

CIAO!
Hello! (also Goodbye!)

CIAO AMICI
Hello my friends

DAI, DAI
Come on!

FINE
The End

GELATO
Ice cream

GRAZIE
Thank you

MAMMA MIA!
Good heavens!

PER CARITÀ
For goodness' sake

PER FAVORE
Please

LE PERSONE
The people

PIAZZA
Public square

PICCOLA
Little one

ROSSO
Red

SBRIGATI
Come on

SCUSI/SCUSA
Excuse me

SEI IN RITARDO!
You're late!

SIGNORA
Madam

SIGNORE E SIGNORI
Ladies and Gentlemen

ROMAN NUMERALS

I = 1, V = 5, X = 10

I = 1
II = 2
III = 3
IV = 4
V = 5

VI = 6
VII = 7
VIII = 8
IX = 9
X = 10

HORACE'S DICTIONARY

Sometimes I have no idea what Horace is talking about, so I thought we should include these explanations of some of his funny expressions. Horace agreed and said, 'I have provided some assistance, in case any of you young whippersnappers have any trouble with my words!'

ABOMINABLE very bad. Terrible!

ACQUAINTANCE a person one knows, but not very well.

AVAUNT go away!

BEHOLD see or observe, especially something or someone impressive. For example, I imagine people often say: Behold the wonderful Horace!

BLITHERING IDIOT blithering means 'complete or utter'… so, this phrase means complete and utter idiot!

BLUNDERING DITHERHEAD blundering means making silly or clumsy mistakes, and ditherhead is a rude but terribly useful insult of my own creation.

BOUNTY a sum of money, a financial reward.

BUCK a fashionable young man.

COMPATRIOT a fellow citizen. Fraser and Megan are compatriots.

CONTEMPLATING thoughtful thinking.

CONTUMELY very insulting language or treatment.

CONVEYED I used this to mean transported or carried to a place.

DASHING attractive and stylish.

DARESAY a word used when you think something is likely to happen. For example: I daresay Harriet and I shall be friends for many years to come.

DISROBING taking off ones clothes. Those poor statues were all disrobed!

ENSEMBLE I used this to mean a fine set of clothes. It could also mean a group of people or things, particularly a group of musicians or performers.

FITZGIBBERS an expression of surprise, of my own creation. For example: Fitzgibbers! Pizza is magnificent!

FLABBERFOUNDED a useful word that Valentina taught me meaning completely astonished. It's a marvellous combination of flabbergasted and dumbfounded.

FORSOOTH Indeed, in truth.

FREQUENTING to often visit a place. I hope I shall be frequenting Rome in the future!

FUSTIAN Feline fustian often refers to a type of

cloth, but I used it to mean worthless. Feline means cat. So, to the lion in the colosseum I said: you worthless cat!

GREAT GRIMALKINS Grimalkin also means cat, so this useful phrase means: Colossal cats!

HITHER towards this place.

INFERNAL irritating and tiresome. You could say: Those infernal Silverbottoms!

INTELLIGENCE often used to mean cleverness or understanding, but I used it to mean secret information.

IMPERTINENT to be rude or not show respect.

NAY no!

NOBLE I used this to mean superior, but it can also mean belonging to wealth or royalty, or having fine qualities.

MERE used to emphasise how small or unimportant someone or something is

MORTAL a human person (as opposed to a statue, like me.)

PASSAGE this can mean several things, but I used it to mean a journey.

POST-HASTE with the

greatest speed!

PREPOSTEROUS similar to ridiculous, impossible, or outrageous.

PRESTIGIOUS something or someone with high status, usually much admired. Like me!

PROWESS to show skill or expertise at something.

RESOLVED determined to do something.

SCURVY SCULLION another insult! In this incident, scurvy means worthless, and scullion means a low ranking servant.

SHENANIGANS mischievous behaviour.

SPLENDIFEROUS Brilliant! Better than brilliant!

STERLING WORK this can refer to British money but I use the word to describe an excellent thing or person. So this phrase means: Excellent job!

TIS it is.

THENCE from that place or time. For example: we went first to the colosseum and thence to the Trevi fountain.

THUNDERSMACKED a useful word that I taught Valentina meaning

completely astonished. It's a marvellous combination of thunderstruck and gobsmacked.

UNCOMMON it can mean unusual or rare, but I tend to mean exceptional or remarkable.

VEXED VERY annoyed.

VOYAGE a long journey.

WHEREUPON after which. For example: I enjoyed several pizzas, whereupon I washed them down with some splendiferous pink lemonade!

WHIPPERSNAPPER a young person who might not know everything.

ZARBLES an expression of surprise, of my own creation. For example: Zarbles! This word is a bit like fitzgibbers!

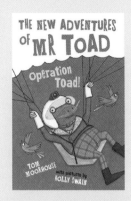

LOVE HORACE AND HARRIET?
WHY NOT TRY THESE TOO!